TO JOSH, ZACH, AND ALLY—MY FIRST READERS, MY STAUNCH
SUPPORTERS, AND MY VERY FAVORITE PEOPLE —B. F.

FOR HOLLY, AND FOR ALL SHARK LOVERS —B. M.

Library of Congress Cataloging-in-Publication Data:
Ferry, Beth, author.

Land shark / by Beth Ferry ; illustrated by Ben Mantle.

pages cm

Summary: Bobby wants a shark for his birthday, so he is disappointed when his parents get him a puppy instead--but this puppy turns out to be a bit of a shark herself.

ISBN 978-1-4521-2458-2

1. Puppies--Juvenile fiction. 2. Birthdays--Juvenile fiction. 3. Gifts--Juvenile fiction. 4. Sharks--Juvenile fiction. [1. Dogs--Fiction. 2. Animals--Infancy--Fiction. 3. Sharks--Fiction. 4. Pets--Fiction.] I. Mantle, Ben, illustrator. II. Title.

PZ7.1.F47Lan 2015

813.6--dc23

2014020021

Manufactured in China.

MIX
Paper from responsible sources
FSC
www.fsc.org
FSC™ C104723

Design by Ryan Hayes.
Typeset in Brandon Text.
The illustrations in this book were rendered in watercolor paint, pencil, and retouched digitally.

10 9 8 7 6

Chronicle Books LLC
680 Second Street
San Francisco, California 94107

Chronicle Books—we see things differently. Become part of our community at www.chroniclekids.com.

LAND SHARK

BY
BETH FERRY

ILLUSTRATED BY
BEN MANTLE

chronicle books·san francisco

Bobby had a plan.

A FISHY plan.

A WISHFUL plan.

A FRIGHTFUL,
BITE-FUL,
DELIGHTFUL
plan.

STEP 1: Convince parents

STEP 2: Get shark

Not a small freshwater shark,
but a real, scooped-out-of-the-ocean,
chock-full-of-teeth shark.

A whale shark

or a lemon shark

or a bull shark.

It didn't matter.
Bobby liked them all.

He baited a hook with clever signs,

pets MAKe the VERY best, Most Coolest birthday Presents EveR!

Ready, set, pet!

and reeled his parents right in.
He forgot just one TINY detail.

On the morning of his birthday, Bobby's parents threw
open the garage door. "Surprise!" they yelled.

No enormous saltwater tank.
No rows of sharp teeth.
No awesome dorsal fin.
No . . . shark.

"HAPPY BIRTHDAY!"

"What's this?" Bobby asked.
"A puppy," said his mom. "The 'very best, most coolest present ever.'"
"Good one, Mom. Are we going to the aquarium?"

"For what?" his dad asked.
"For my shark," Bobby answered.
"Don't be silly," said his mom.
"You can't have a shark."
"Sharks aren't pets," his sister said.
"Did you think you were getting a shark?" his brother laughed.

Bobby ran up to his room, not crying, not crying one salty tear.
Shark lovers did not cry.

His mom brought the puppy upstairs.
"Look at her," she crooned.
"She's sweet,"
Sharks aren't sweet.
"and adorable,"
Sharks are not adorable.
"and cuddly."
Sharks do not cuddle.
"Just give her a chance."

Shark lovers cannot be converted to dog lovers. EVER!

The next day, Bobby awoke to shouting and barking.

"Have you seen my shoe?" his dad called.

"Have you seen my baseball?" his brother yelled.

"Panda?" his sister cried. "Has anyone seen Panda?"

The puppy dropped Panda at Bobby's feet, tail wagging.
Bobby surveyed the damage.

It was DESTRUCTION, with a capital D.

It was frightful.
It was bite-ful.
It was delightful!

He could hear his mother coming.
"Good luck," he told the puppy.

After one week, the puppy had chewed through five pairs of shoes, six stuffed animals, and the legs of three chairs.
She barked at 10 p.m., 2 a.m., and any other "m" she wanted.

"SHHHH . . . ," said Bobby's sister.

"ARK!" said the puppy.

"SHHHH . . . ," said Bobby's brother.

"ARK!" said the puppy.

"SHHHH . . ." "ARK!"

"I wish," said Bobby.

Everyone was grumpy.

Everyone except Bobby.
He was thrilled.
A shark was looking
better and better.

That night, the doorbell rang.
"Is this yours?" Mrs. Grenly asked,
pointing at a pile of garbage.
The garbage ran right over to Bobby.
He sniffed.

"She must have smelled your spaghetti sauce. Did you know that sharks have an amazing sense of smell?"

Mrs. Grenly peered into the house. "Do you have a shark in there?" "Not yet," said Bobby.

Bobby's mom handed him the puppy,
"Someone needs to give her a bath."
"Or give her away," Bobby mumbled.

But as he carried the puppy upstairs, he
whispered, "Tiger sharks like garbage too."
The puppy licked his face then splashed
into the tub.

Bobby turned away.
Shark lovers can**NOT**
be converted to dog lovers.

No matter how
great they swim.

On Saturday morning, Bobby
awoke to a scratching sound.
He opened his door and the
puppy charged in. She sniffed
his rug, sniffed his clothes,
and barked at his posters.

She scooted under the bed and grabbed Toothy.
"Don't . . ." Bobby began, but it was too late.
"Stop!" he yelled, lunging for Toothy.
The puppy pulled.
Bobby tugged.
The puppy growled.
Bobby yelled, "Drop it. Drop it now."

The puppy dropped it.
Then she took a
GREAT BIG CHOMP
out of it.
Bobby gasped.

The puppy trotted over
and dropped the head
at Bobby's feet.
Then she wagged her tail.

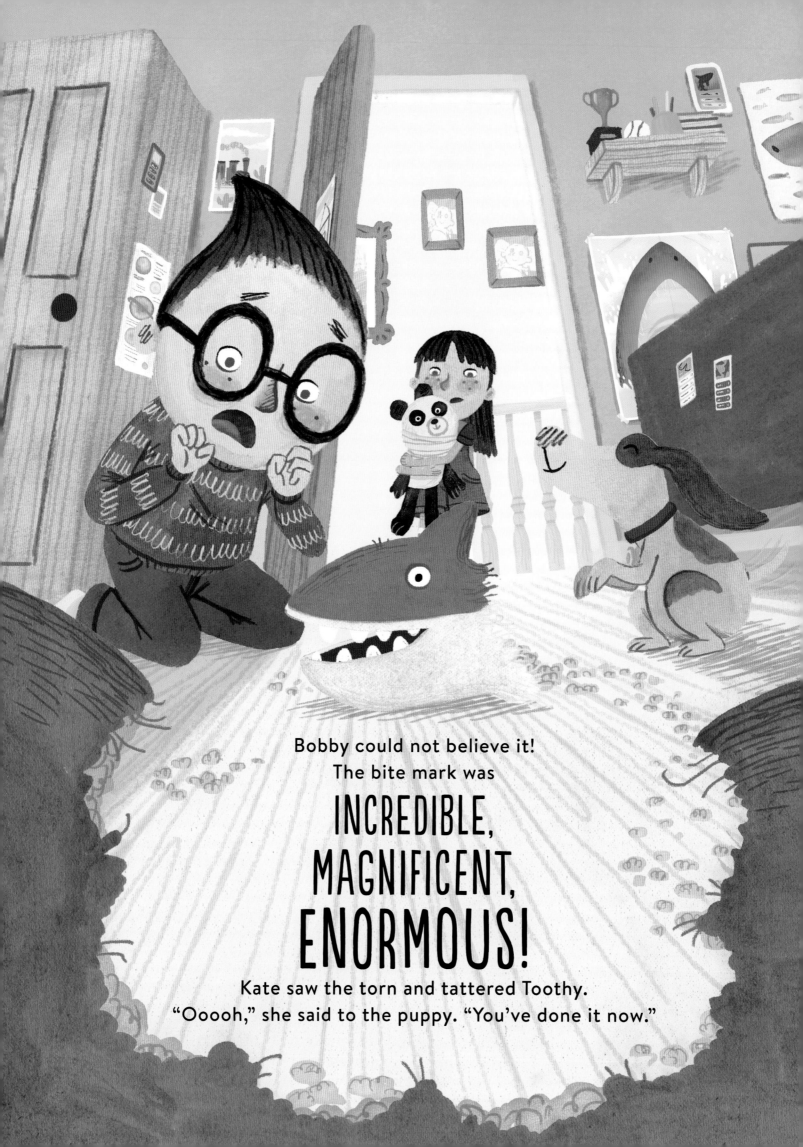

Bobby could not believe it!
The bite mark was

INCREDIBLE,
MAGNIFICENT,
ENORMOUS!

Kate saw the torn and tattered Toothy.
"Ooooh," she said to the puppy. "You've done it now."

And the puppy **HAD** done it.
She had barked and chewed and bitten her way . . .
right into Bobby's heart.

Bobby was a shark lover.
And shark lovers, as it turns out,
CAN be converted to dog lovers.
In fact, they can love lots of amazing things.

And with less than a year
until his next birthday,
Bobby had a plan.

A **FANTASTIC** plan.
A **JURASSIC** plan.
A **FRIGHTFUL,
BITE-FUL,
DELIGHTFUL**
plan.

STEP 1: Convince parents
STEP 2:...

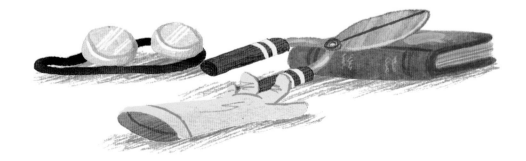